THREE
MAGIC BALLS

BY RICHARD EGIELSKI

A LAURA GERINGER BOOK
An Imprint of HarperCollinsPublishers

After school, Tuesdays and Fridays, Rudy worked at Uncle Dinkleschmidt's rare and antique toy shop.

One afternoon, an old woman came into the shop carrying three rubber balls in a glass box. Each ball had a brightly painted face.

"I want to sell these," she said. "They're too much trouble for me."

"Not for me," said Uncle Dinkleschmidt, winking at Rudy. Rudy thought he saw one of the balls wink too.

Uncle Dinkleschmidt bought the balls and put them in his special display case.

"Will you take good care of them?" the lady asked Rudy, as she placed a gold whistle in his hand and disappeared, right on the spot!

Rudy, stunned, couldn't utter a sound.

"I have to go to the dentist now," said Uncle Dinkleschmidt. "Please mind the shop, Rudy, and remember—don't play with the toys."

Absentmindedly, Rudy put the whistle in his pocket and got back to work. Soon he felt someone staring at him, and then he heard voices whisper, "Come. . . . Come. . . . Come."

Was he dreaming? Louder they said, "Take. . . .
Take. . . . Take."

Rudy opened Uncle Dinkleschmidt's special display
case and took the balls out. "BOUNCE! BOUNCE!
BOUNCE!" they shouted. He bounced a ball.

As it hit the floor, up popped a large rubber man.

The rubber man grabbed the other two balls and
bounced them.
   "Now meet my brothers!" he said with a laugh.

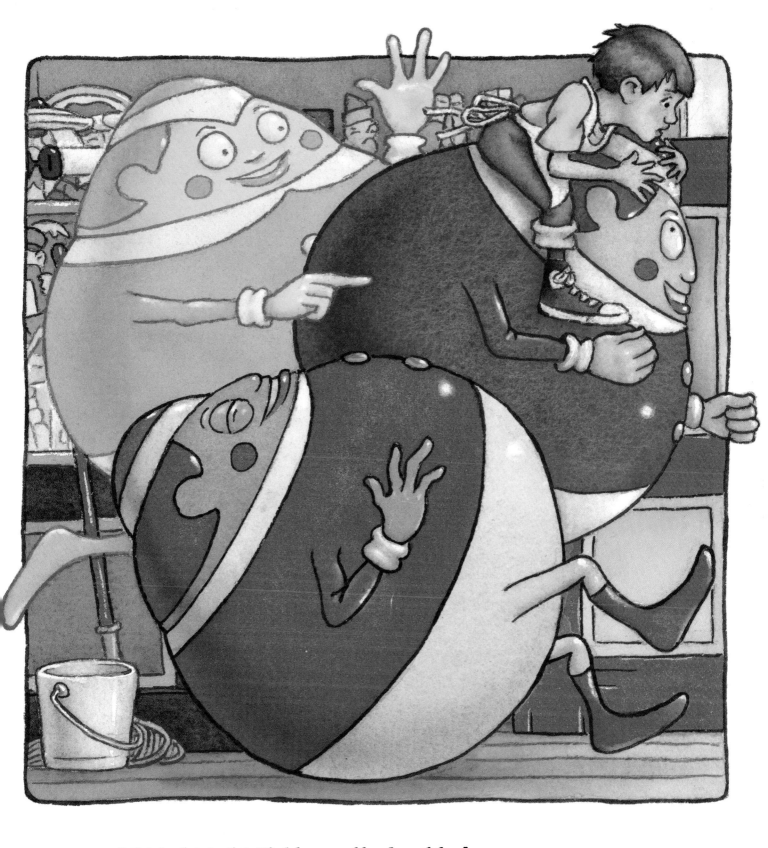

"GO! GO! GO!" they all chuckled.
And taking Rudy along, they went bouncing out of
the shop.

They bounced down the street . . .

up past the buildings . . .

and into the sky.

Suddenly, out of the blue, came an airplane,
careening out of control.
   "HELP!" yelled the pilot.

"Save that plane!" Rudy shouted.
Instantly, the ball brothers sprang into action.

The first one slowed the plane down.

The second smothered the smoking engine.

The third softened the landing.

"Thank you!" said the pilot.
"Thank you!" said the crew.
"Thank you!" said all the passengers.
"You're welcome," Rudy replied. "But I really have
to get back to work now."

"Waa! Waa! Waa!" cried the ball brothers. "We're ruined!"

"I'm too skinny!" said the first.

"I'm too fat!" said the second.

"I'm too flat!" wailed the third.

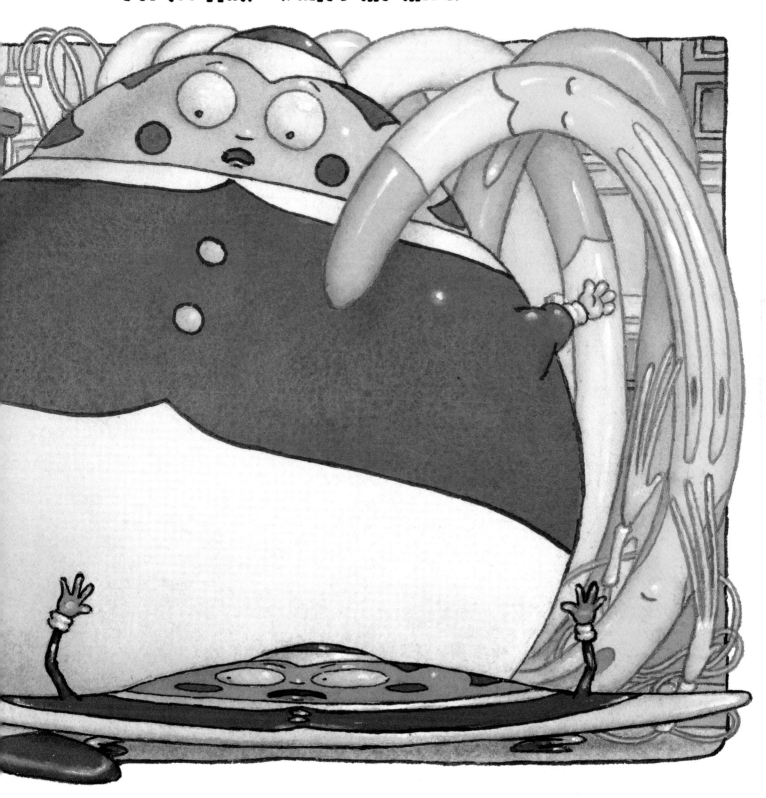

"BOUNCE! BOUNCE! BOUNCE!" they all cried. But they couldn't bounce.
"Quiet please. I can't think," said Rudy.

But they cried even louder. "WAA! WAA! WAA!"
"QUIET!" Rudy shouted. Then, remembering the
gold whistle still in his pocket, he took it out and blew
it. BRRRRRRR!

With a shiver and a shake, the flat ball brother
shrank back into a ball.

Rudy blew his whistle two more times.

Quickly, Rudy gathered up the balls and raced
back to the shop.
    He arrived only seconds before Uncle Dinkleschmidt.

"Some kind of commotion out there," mumbled Uncle
Dinkleschmidt.

On payday, Rudy bought the three magic balls.

"I can't blame you for wanting these," said Uncle Dinkleschmidt. "Those faces. You can almost hear them speak."

"Almost," Rudy said, smiling.

For Irwin Greenberg and
Bela Rosenkranz,
2 magic teachers

Three Magic Balls
Copyright © 2000 by Richard Egielski
Printed in the U.S.A. All rights reserved.
http://www.harperchildrens.com

Library of Congress Cataloging-in-Publication Data
Egielski, Richard.
  Three magic balls / by Richard Egielski.
      p.   cm.
  Summary: After an old woman sells three unusual balls to the
owner of the toy shop where Rudy works, she gives him a golden
whistle that comes in very handy when the balls lead him on a
magical adventure.
  ISBN 0-06-026032-7. — ISBN 0-06-026033-5 (lib. bdg.)
  [1. Magic—Fiction.]   I. Title.
PZ7.E3215Th   2000   99-30278
[E]—dc21   CIP
                                                                  AC

Typography by Alicia Mikles
1   2   3   4   5   6   7   8   9   10
❖
First Edition